Second Chance in Pumpkin City

Sarah Lamb

Paperback ISBN: 978-1-960418-02-9

Contents

1. Chapter 1   1

2. Chapter 2   11

3. Chapter 3   17

4. Chapter 4   25

5. Chapter 5   33

6. Chapter 6   39

7. Chapter 7   43

8. Chapter 8   49

9. Chapter 9   55

10. Chapter 10   61

11. Chapter 11   65

12. Chapter 12   71

13. Chapter 13   75

14. Chapter 14   81

15. Chapter 15   87

16. Chapter 16   95

17. Epilogue   101

Chapter 1

Kelly Wilson slammed on the brakes as a horse wandered onto the road. She waited, tapping her fingers against the steering wheel as another joined it, then two more. They didn't seem in any hurry to cross. Once the roadway was clear, she inched forward slowly, then stopped again, as Mr. Grayson emerged from the side of the road just ahead, shaking a bucket of feed and the horses hurried in front of her car again, back in the direction they'd come from.

Mr. Grayson gave her a grin and a wave, and after returning it, Kelly started on her way again. She liked Mr. Grayson. A local Amish farmer and jack-of-all-trades, he had helped her parents many times. His work was excellent, and somehow, he managed to do it all without electric power tools. Being Amish, he used either hand tools or else ones that ran off compressed air. It always amazed her how much he could do with seemingly old-fashioned ways.

The radio got staticky as Kelly turned down the small highway. Scanning for a new station, but not finding any, she sighed. That was one thing about living in a small town. No good radio or TV over the air signals. Giving up, she listened to the voice fading in and out before she got tired of it and clicked the radio off.

It was a beautiful day. The sun was bright in the cloudless sky, and the faint smell of mid-summer lilac mixed with manure from a farmer fertilizing his field drifted in her open car window. What a combination! Even as she scrunched her nose she smiled. Kelly slowed as she passed a field of Jersey cows. She'd actually missed them. That slow amble they did was kind of relaxing. It was nice to be back home for a few days.

She pushed a strand of blonde hair behind her ear, clicked on her turn signal, and maneuvered down another road. It had been a while since she'd passed another car, but she still drove carefully, mindful of the fact that horse and buggies might be traveling the same way as her—only much slower.

Having grown up in Pumpkin City, she'd actually been anxious to leave the small, sleepy town, but once she'd gone off to college where it was hectic, fast-paced, and a little too crowded at times, daydreams kept filling her mind with memories of Pumpkin City's wide-open pastures, slower way of living, and the hardworking people who lived there.

In the city, such things as honesty boxes, a container set out where passersby would pay for their purchases at an unattended roadside produce or baked good stands, were nonexistent. Most people didn't smile or wave as they went past like they did here, and you could work with someone for six months and still not know their name. In Pumpkin City, everyone knew everyone.

In fact, everyone knew everyone's business too. It didn't matter if you were Plain people, the Amish wearing simple clothes, long dresses, and bonnets or hats riding around in buggies, or the other residents, those wearing jeans and shorter skirts and driving cars, if there was a bit of news, before the sun set, everyone seemed to know it.

It wasn't always a bad thing though. The community really rallied around its members. From missing animals to escaped herds, a field that needed to be plowed or funds that needed to be raised for someone sick, residents chipping in with their time and efforts if they could. She'd even been the recipient of that once, when her kitten, Chocolate, had gone missing. Within a day, an Amish girl had brought her back, Chocolate having wandered over to a nearby farm. She'd been so grateful to have her fluffy, light-brown furball back.

Kelly navigated into the small neighborhood, heading to her childhood home. She was glad to see not much had changed, even though it had been a few months since she'd been there. Her job as a receptionist at a real estate office made her take in the neighborhood with fresh eyes. Curb appeal, expansive trees, beautiful scenery. This place had it all. She could almost hear one of the agents talking in her mind, and it made her smile. Soon, she was going to be one of the agents. A top agent. Nothing was going to stand in her way of that. She had the focus, the drive, and the determination to make sure nothing, and no one stopped her.

Pulling into the driveway of her parent's house, Kelly stood and stretched, and out of habit glanced around her to see who was outside to wave at.

Then she turned right back around and stared at her shoes, trying to get her temper under control.

You have got to be kidding me. What is he doing here?

Yanking her bag out of the backseat, Kelly jogged up to the front door, anxious to get inside. The yellow door was opened by her mom before she got there.

"Hi, sweetie! Oh, look at you!" her mom said, nearly crushing her in a hug.

"Hi, Mom!" Kelly answered, trying to squeeze past to get inside. Somehow, her mom knew. She didn't budge.

"Did you see who else was home for the weekend?" her mom asked, just a hint of a song in her voice.

"Yes. I saw. Now can I come in?" Kelly wasn't trying to sound childish, but every time she thought about Brett Hiser she just wanted to punch him in the gut. Maybe that pretty-boy nose, too.

If she wasn't worried about breaking her knuckles, maybe she would.

All through high school, it was assumed that she and Brett, who everyone called the perfect couple, would get married and live happily ever after. That might have happened too. If it weren't for Megan Hollister. The person she *thought* was her best friend. Miss Perfect, who not only stole her boyfriend, but had also landed a full ride scholarship to one of the top schools in the state. Meanwhile, Kelly had to work her way through school and take out student loans she was worried about paying back.

Kelly had stumbled upon the two of them in a very compromising position, and even though her mom told her she ought to hear Brett's side of the story, she wasn't interested. Nothing he, or Megan, could have said would have changed anything. She knew what she saw. There was no excuse good enough to make her forgive either of them.

She gave Brett back the necklace he'd given her, changed her cellphone number, and the next day left for college, not once looking back. She couldn't. It was too painful how he had betrayed her. The two of them had grown up together. They'd been in every grade, almost every sport, gone to every event together.

You thought you knew a person...

Kelly shook herself out of her thoughts. "Where's Dad?" she asked, setting down her bag in the living room. She spotted Chocolate sleeping in a sunbeam and give her a head rub.

Her mom shook her head and quirked her lips. "He's out back, obsessing over his flowers for the show at the end of summer fair. Mildred down the street won last year, and he's determined not to get second place this year."

Kelly laughed. For as long as she could remember, her dad and the woman down the street had been in a battle for who would get the first-place ribbon with their flowers. The prize usually alternated between the two of them, and she wondered what would happen if a third person became a serious contestant. Her dad had the same competitive streak as she did.

"What did he plant again?" she asked. "Was it chrysanthemums?"

"Uh huh," her mom said. She raised her eyebrows. "You'd think he was Scrooge protecting his gold coins the way he checks those flowers. I think it's the seventh time today, and it's only three in the afternoon."

"I heard that," Kelly's dad said, walking in. "And Scrooge never had to fight powdery mildew. It's all over our tomatoes! It might attack my mums! But how's my girl?" he asked, wrapping an arm around Kelly.

"Hi Dad! Doing good," Kelly giggled. "Sounds like you've grown a winner this year."

"I hope so. Someone has to show that woman down the street she's got competition," her dad said, flexing his muscles. "I'm glad you're here to see my hopeful victory over her peonies. They look sharp this year. She's mixing her own fertilizer. Can you believe it? I'm going to do that next year. By the way, did you see who else came to town for the fair?"

"Yes." Kelly gave her parents a look, and they shrugged. What a question. Of course she noticed him. Everyone noticed Brett. He was tall, good-looking, and...and in the past.

"Just saying, that's all," her dad said, holding up his hands. "Though, don't be rude to Brett later when he stops by, okay? I need his help."

"Stops by? What are you talking about?" Kelly asked. A frown formed. This visit home wasn't going like she'd planned.

"Oh, didn't I mention?" her mom said, in a tone that sounded a little too casual. "Brett's coming by for an early dinner."

"Uh no, no he's not," Kelly said and crossed her arms. "Why would you invite him?"

"Simple," her dad said. "Come here with me and you'll see why. Dinner's just a bribe. And a thank you."

Kelly nodded and followed him, but paused, as through the window she saw Brett. He was mowing the lawn for his parents, and had stopped for a moment to drink from a bottle of water. His t-shirt was damp and clung to his chest. Somehow, he looked the same as she remembered, just more filled out. His arms and chest were muscular, but not so large to be unattractive. He must have a ton of girls after him.

She'd Facebook stalked him, but had never seen who he was going out with now, even though he had a ton of messages from one girl in particular, Wendy. He kept his social media pretty quiet with public updates, but that didn't stop her from checking on it every few weeks. She knew she shouldn't, but even though more than four years had passed, she hadn't moved on from their relationship. Somehow, she couldn't.

Dating other guys just didn't have the same comfortable familiarity, the spark of excitement, the same interesting conversations. No matter how many times she'd tried to make a connection with someone new, she never bothered with a second date. At this rate, her roommate told her, she was likely going to be alone forever.

The thought made her angry, and she knew the only person to blame if that did happen was Brett. And definitely Megan. Each time she thought about the two of them, her emotions ranged from being angry to heartbroken to feeling sick to her stomach. It didn't matter all that time had passed, it feelings today were as raw as they'd been the first time.

Was it because she'd thought they were always going to be together and she didn't want to be hurt again? Was it because there was no closure? Or was it just because Brett was a jerk who had ruined her life?

Chapter 2

Brett shut off the lawnmower and wiped his arm across his forehead. As usual, July was feeling pretty brutal. He looked up as his mom walked out of the house with a bottle of water.

"Thanks for doing this," she said. "Since your dad broke his arm, it's a lot harder for him to do some things."

"No problem," Brett shrugged. "Do I still get ten bucks like I did when I was a kid?"

His mom laughed, and she started to answer when her eyes widened. "Oh! Look who else is home!"

Brett turned his head and sighed. Kelly. Great. The last time he'd tried to talk to her, she punched him. If he thought about it, his nose still hurt. The way she'd shaken her hand afterward and then cradled it made him know it had hurt her too.

"I wonder if her dad knew she was coming home when he asked me over to move that stuff in his garage," he sighed.

His mom looked at him sympathetically. "You know, sweetie, it's been a few years. You two had been friends since you were both in diapers. I don't know what happened, and you don't have to tell me, but isn't it time that you at least mend fences? Being upset at each other doesn't do either of you any good."

Brett threw his hands up. "Tell her that! I tried."

"If something is important, then keep trying," his mom said. "She's stubborn."

That was an understatement. Kelly was whatever it was beyond stubborn. She'd always been that way. In kindergarten, if she wanted a certain color crayon, she was going to do whatever it took to get it, even if it meant multiple timeouts for her behavior. That didn't change as she got older, either. Kelly was competitive, and that made her both a great athlete, and a little difficult to get along with at times. She had a quick temper. She also jumped to conclusions a lot and had a defensive personality.

None of that had ever bothered Brett, because he'd also seen her nice side, her generous side, which not a lot of people knew about.

Sure, she always wanted to be first at everything, but Kelly also paid attention to those around her. When one of their classmates was obviously going through a hard time, Kelly skipped lunches for a few weeks, pretending she wasn't hungry to give hers to the other kid until things got better for him. She also made friends easily, even if she was friends with the guys more than the girls. Brett never minded though, because all the guys knew that Kelly was his.

They'd made it official in high school their junior year, but everyone had known that Kelly and Brett were inseparable long before that.

That had all changed though, the night before Kelly had left for college, and all the plans the two of them had made together had gone up in a poof of smoke.

Brett finished the water and the mowing, then went inside to shower. Rummaging through his duffel bag, he pulled out a clean outfit and thundered down the stairs. His dad was watching an old western, and Brett plopped on the couch next to him.

"How you feeling?" he asked.

"Like an idiot," his dad said. "I mean, how do you trip on the sidewalk and break your arm?"

"Dunno," Brett shrugged. "But I can come back next weekend and mow again if you want."

His dad shook his head. "Nah, I'll find someone. You've got that fancy smanchy job. Can't miss too many days."

Brett laughed. Fancy smanchy didn't exactly describe the office environment with food wrappers and coffee cups littering desks, or the long hours he put in at the IT department, but he enjoyed it. A recruiter had picked him up his junior year from the semi-local state university, when he'd developed a productivity software that his professor encouraged him to enter into a contest. When it won, it not only got snapped up by the government, but he landed the job with one of their contractors, too.

"If you need me, I'll come," he promised. "Family first."

"Doug's going to help me," his dad said, waving his good hand in the direction of Kelly's house. "That's why I offered your help moving all that stuff."

Brett groaned. So that's how he got volunteered. He was a trade.

"What? You don't like the Wilsons?" His dad raised an eyebrow at him, then turned back to the screen as cowboys started riding into town.

"That's not it, Dad, you know that. It's Kelly."

"What about her?" his dad asked, turning down the TV as a shootout started and cowboys started shouting and saloon girls started running for cover.

"She's home," Brett said.

"Ooops. Sorry."

Brett shrugged and stood. "No problem. She'll probably hide from me the whole time. Unless she just stands there glaring at me."

"Maybe she'd like to go with you to the fair. You two always used to go together."

"I don't know," Brett answered, rubbing his chin. He wasn't feeling confident in that, and honestly, as hurt as he was over her dumping him suddenly, he wasn't sure he even wanted to try and have a relationship with her again, friendly or more.

When he saw his dad was still staring at him, waiting for an answer, he nodded. "Maybe. Okay, see ya, I better get helping."

"Wait, you still have that sports app on your phone?" his dad asked. "Show me how that works again."

Brett pulled out his phone and walked his dad through the app. Leaving his dad happily watching the standoff between the cattle rustler and the white hatted sheriff while browsing sports stats, he pulled on his sneakers, double knotting them. The Wilsons had steep steps leading to their basement, and the last thing he wanted was to trip and join his dad in the broken arm club.

A few seconds later, he left the house and paused at the back door. From there he could see the Wilson's garage. The door was open, and Kelly was standing there with her dad. So much for her hiding.

"Better get it over with," he muttered. "But if she tries to punch me again, I'm not going to just stand there and take it."

Chapter 3

Kelly followed her dad out to the garage. When he opened the doors, her jaw dropped. "What's all this?"

"This, is stuff that needs to be moved to the basement," her dad said. "Hence the buttering up of Brett. Some of these boxes are pretty heavy. Even for me. We need young backs for this stuff."

Stuff was an understatement. The entire garage was bursting. Tall stacks of boxes teetered, and though Kelly turned her head this way and that, she couldn't see anything behind the massive cardboard wall that seemed to fill every inch of space.

Her mom joined them. "We just can't do it, sweetie. Not with my back and your dad's blood pressure. He's not supposed to be exerting himself. And you had offered to take a few things down for us."

"Yeah, a few," Kelly said, turning to her parents. "This is a little more than I imagined. How far back does this go?"

"That's why we thought we'd ask Brett to help," her dad explained proudly. "Less for you to do. With the two of you moving it all, it shouldn't take you more than an hour or two. Maybe three. Four?"

Kelly gritted her teeth. "I can do it. I don't need help," she said, even if it wasn't completely true.

I'd do anything not to have to spend time with that jerk again.

"Don't be silly," her mom said. "Brett's here and can help."

"Sure can," a voice came from behind them. "Anything for a neighbor."

Kelly turned, her eyes shooting daggers. Brett stood with a grin on his face, looking every bit as good looking as she had remembered. Maybe more. He waved to her parents, who seemed to light up when they saw him. They'd always loved Brett. Who didn't?

Her, that's who. Kelly frowned and crossed her arms. *How dare he? He should be suffering and miserable and ashamed to show his face around me after what he did.*

Kelly took a deep breath and looked back at the garage. "Do you want me to get started?" she asked, ignoring Brett. She could sense him coming closer. The smell of his aftershave made her swallow hard. It was warm, and spicy, and...

Stop that. He's a two-timing jerk, remember?

"No, no, not yet," Kelly's mom said. "Let's have dinner. It won't take me long to finish up. I'm practically done."

"You are?" Kelly crinkled her nose. "I didn't smell anything when I walked in." She sniffed the air again. "Do you want some help?"

"No, no, I have this," her mom assured her. She tapped a button on her cellphone. As she walked away, Kelly could hear her say, "Hello, I need to place a delivery order."

Kelly couldn't help it, she smiled and shook her head. Her mom was a fantastic cook, but she couldn't blame her for wanting to do something different. After so many decades of cooking, who wouldn't want to do take out when possible?

She half listened to her dad as he asked how Brett's family was doing. It seemed Brett's dad had broken his arm, and her dad had been helping with things around their house, like mowing. She wanted to ask how he was, Brett's dad had been like her second father, but she didn't want to talk to Brett. No one could hold a grudge like she could. And this wasn't one she wanted to let go of.

Every time she thought about coming around the corner and seeing Brett with his arms wrapped around Megan, and her clinging to him... If this were a cartoon, smoke would be coming out of her ears. Kelly reached over and grabbed a box.

"Wait, pumpkin," her dad said. "Like your mom said. Let's eat first."

Kelly nodded and set it down. "I'll go help Mom," she said, and went inside the house. If the door slammed a little, well, that wasn't her fault. The old screen door always slammed. But if she'd pulled it open extra hard, well...she was mad. She wanted to enjoy her visit home and the annual summer fair. Not be surrounded by *him* every minute of it.

Her mom was in the kitchen, half inside the fridge. "Want some help?" Kelly asked.

"Sure," her mom said. "I thought we'd eat on the screened-in porch. Want to take the two liters out? I've already got cups and napkins out there."

Kelly nodded, plugged her phone into the charger on the counter, and wrapped her arms around the sodas to carry them all at once. Her favorite was there, and so was Brett's. She sighed. Of course it was. Her mom was nothing, if not polite. She wasn't looking forward to the meal, though. Hopefully she could avoid having a conversation with him.

Stepping into the screened-in porch, Kelly couldn't help but feel relaxed, almost all at once. For a brief moment, Brett was forgotten. She loved this room. The whole family did. Her mom had saved up for a long time to build it, and then the outdoor furniture was bought slowly, a few pieces at a time. Now, it was an oasis.

There were four ratan chairs with thick cushions, two loveseats, a low table, several plants that hung from the ceiling or were on stands, and a ceiling fan with a light built in. Best of all, it was bug free. No gnats, no mosquitoes, no wasps or bees or flies. It was a completely bug free zone.

There was the sound of a car, and Kelly peered through the screen to see who was pulling up. It was the delivery driver. Her stomach rumbled when she saw where it was from. It had been too long since she'd had Sergio's subs. She jogged into the house to help her mom.

The smell of the freshly baked bread combined with the different toppings and the crisp French fries, made her mouth water. Her dad and Brett came inside too.

"Thank you so much," Brett said, hugging her mom. "I love that place."

"Is there anyone who doesn't?" Kelly's mom asked. "Let's go in the back."

They sat with her parents in two chairs on one side of the low table. That meant she'd have to sit next to Brett. Great. That said, sitting next to him meant she didn't have to look at him. Kelly sat across from her mom. Ignoring Brett, she grabbed for her food.

"So Brett," her dad started. "Tell us how the new job is."

Kelly pretended not to listen, but she didn't miss the excitement in Brett's voice as he explained his job. It sounded like it was made just for him. She couldn't help but feel a tiny bit glad for him. He always wanted to work in the government sector, and now he was.

She dabbed a fry in ketchup, washed it down with some soda, and nearly spit it all out as her mom asked, "And what about your girlfriend?"

Chapter 4

Kelly started sputtering, and Brett could only imagine it was because of the large bites she'd taken. Half her sandwich was already gone. The girl didn't eat, she inhaled. Always had.

She held up her hand, her eyes watering, and gasped, "I'm fine. Wrong way down."

"Ahh," Brett turned back to ask, "Sorry, what was the question?"

"Your girlfriend. Tell us about her," Kelly's mom said.

A set up. This was absolutely a set up. He just wondered if both of their mothers were involved. Could they be any more obvious about trying to push him and Kelly together?

Brett wasn't sure how to answer. Kelly was paying close attention and for a moment, he thought about making up a story just to get back at her, but that wasn't who he was. He gave a little shrug and went for the truth.

"Actually, I don't have a girlfriend anymore," he said. "My job keeps me pretty busy and it wouldn't be fair to one that I'm not able to commit right now." His thoughts drifted to Wendy, an old classmate, who never seemed to stop messaging him, even though he ignored them, completely uninterested in her.

"But what about you, Kelly?" he asked, unable to resist the tease. "Seeing anyone right now?"

There. He could play at this game too.

Kelly glared at him, her mouth full, and as she swallowed, Brett could tell she didn't like the three sets of eyes staring at her. Finally, she said, "I've been on quite a few dates, but if I want to be chosen to become a real estate agent, I have to prove my worth. I'm shadowing two other agents right now," she explained, looking at her parents.

"That just started this week, but I have to be 100% available at any time. They knew I was coming here this weekend, but I'm not sure when the next weekend will be that I can. Weekends are the busiest time of the week for house hunting."

Her parents nodded. They asked her a follow up question and Brett let his mind drift. A lot of dates, huh? With who, he wondered. She was living in a large city, one probably filled with plenty of good looking guys who were loaded. Especially if she was in real estate. Maybe she was even seeing the boss.

Brett didn't like that idea. It made him feel angry, which he also didn't like. He'd always loved Kelly. He still did, really, if he admitted it. Not seeing her for more than four years didn't change the fact they'd been best friends and dated. The two of them had been inseparable. They still should be. Maybe his mom was right, and it was time to try and reconnect, or at least be friends again.

But that all depended on if Kelly agreed, and if he could get over feeling hurt.

Even though he wasn't too thrilled about being on the spot right now, it was kind of funny watching her squirm. And maybe they could mend a few fences this weekend. The idea wasn't a bad one. It would be nice to at least know where things stood between them. Right now, he wasn't sure.

Even if it was her hot head that broke them up, he was willing to try to put the past aside for the sake of old times. Brett studied Kelly for a moment. Though several years had passed, she looked pretty much the same. Jeans, a casual T, her hair in a ponytail. He wondered if her personality had changed any. He could tell she was still stubborn, but had she softened any?

Kelly reached past him for the Dr. Pepper, and he caught a familiar scent. She was still using strawberry shampoo. He wanted to lean in, to breathe in deeply. It wasn't fair. Kelly had never given him a chance to explain. Not that he could. He wasn't going to share something Megan had asked him to keep secret. But she didn't even try to let him explain. It was like...she wanted to walk away. Was that it? She was off to college and didn't want to be tied down?

Standing abruptly, Brett grabbed his trash. When everyone looked at his sudden movement, he grinned, "If I don't get moving on those boxes, I'm going to be too tired to lift a thing after that meal," he said.

When Kelly also started to stand, he shook his head. "You finish. There's no rush. There are tons of boxes and they are going anywhere unless we move them." *And really, I want a few minutes by myself.*

He left the room, pitched his garbage in the kitchen trash can and stood, looking at the towering boxes. There were so many, he wasn't sure the best place to start, without knocking over a stack. A shadow formed, and he looked over his shoulder. Kelly's dad shrugged, looking a little embarrassed. "I'm sorry."

"Don't be. A good workout," Brett said.

"Not the boxes," her dad answered. "Though... yeah. It's a lot, I know. When my business closed..." he stopped, then shook his head, "I couldn't just let it all go. I'm going to reopen one day, once..."

Brett put his hand on Doug's shoulder. "No problem," he said. He knew about the business. There was no need to make him relive the experience. One of Doug's consultants for his construction company had taken been skimming from them for years. He was so sneaky, he'd taken more than a million dollars from various companies, including the Wilsons small one.

The guy went to prison, but didn't repay anything. As a result, most of the businesses, being smaller, closed. Doug was now working at a local hardware store and hating every minute of it. The Wilsons nearly lost all they had, and were slowly rebuilding. Things like that took time though, and it sure wasn't easy.

Her dad cleared his throat. "I mean Kelly. You know how the women are," he said, motioning between their two houses. "Still want to fix you two up. Patch the holes."

"Yeah." Brett sighed and rubbed his hand though his hair. "I just want to be friends at least. That's all I need. I don't like people being upset at me. Especially when I didn't do anything wrong."

"Life's unfair sometimes," Doug agreed, his hands in his pockets.

They stood there for a moment, reflecting. With Doug's sad expression, Brett was sure he was thinking about his business.

Footsteps sounded and Kelly walked in. Brett didn't look at her. The crushing weight in his heart was just too much. He hadn't expected all the feelings of missing her to resurface once he'd seen her.

Clearing his throat, he went to the box closest to him. "Where do you want them?" he asked, gesturing to the boxes. "Basement?"

"Yes. Just stack them there."

Kelly grabbed a box and left the garage. Brett reached for one as Doug added, "We'll be back in a while. We're going to go drop off my entry into the flower contest."

"Good luck," Brett grinned. "You'll get it this year, I just know it."

"Sure hope so. And listen, the basement door isn't acting right. Don't let it shut, or you might get locked in. I haven't had time to look at it."

"Thanks for the heads up," Brett said, hoisting the heavy box onto his shoulder. He turned and went into the house, passing Kelly coming from the other direction. He grinned at her, thinking about making a joke, of being the first to talk to the other and try and remove a little of the tension clouding around her, but she ignored him. He grimaced.

Fine by me. I'm just here to help her dad and leave.

Maybe mending fences wasn't on the weekend agenda. Brett carefully navigated down the steep steps of the basement. He spotted where Kelly had started a pile and set his box next to hers. As he turned, he heard Kelly's steps at the top of the stairs.

"Hey, your dad said—"

"You know what?" Kelly stopped, leaning up against the door and glared at him. "I don't really want to talk to you. Let's just move these boxes and you can go home, okay?"

She pushed forward, and the door started to close.

"Catch it!" Brett hollered, pointing.

Kelly turned to see where he was motioning to, and the door shut with a click.

Chapter 5

Brett rushed up the stairs and started pulling on the door. "What's the big deal?" Kelly asked. "Just open it."

"That's what I was trying to tell you," Brett growled. "But of course, you didn't want to listen. You never do." His eyes were so angry looking that she took a step back. "Your dad said not to let the door shut, it might not open again. There's a problem with it."

"So? We just call for help." Kelly handed Brett the box she was holding and knocked on the door. "Hello! Dad? Mom? We're stuck!"

She kept banging, calling loudly, but no one came.

"They might not be home," Brett said, and walked the box down the stairs. "Your dad said they were going to take over his flower to the festival."

Kelly groaned. "If that's the case, they'll be gone for hours. Dad will start talking with the woman down the street. They'll ask each other about their fertilizer, talk about bugs and soil and all that other stuff, and then they'll start walking around looking at all the other entries. They won't get back for ages."

She banged louder on the door. "Help! Mom! Dad!" After a solid minute, she gave up. "That's not going to work."

Her face brightened and she reached for her back pocket. "My phone! I'll just call. I should have thought of that sooner." She felt around for the familiar lump. "Umm. Uh oh." Frantically she patted each of her pockets, then with a groan remembered where it was. Sitting on the kitchen counter.

Swiveling her head, looking for another idea, Kelly saw Brett staring at her. "What?" she asked.

"Do you have your phone?" he asked.

"No. It's in the kitchen. Do you?" she asked hopefully.

"Nope. Dad was using it to look up sports stats. He was enjoying himself so much, I just let him have it."

"Figures," Kelly muttered.

"You should have let me talk," Brett said. "I tried to tell you." He stepped closer. "Let me look again."

He pushed against the door and tugged on the doorknob. Leaning close, he examined the latch and the doorframe. After a moment, he backed up. Sighing, he said, "Yep. It's locked or jammed or something."

"Really? I didn't realize that," Kelly said sarcastically. She pushed past him and started rummaging around in the basement.

"What are you doing?" Brett asked.

"Looking for a way to get us out of here," she said. *This would never have happened if he weren't here. Maybe.*

Kelly rummaged through a box. Surely there were tools or something. Of course, they had to be the only house she knew of with a basement that was fully underground. No window at all to shout through, no door that led to outside. If they could just call for help, they'd get out. Eventually. And not soon enough for her.

Kelly huffed out a breath. "Okay then. Looks like we are stuck until someone comes along or we find a way out. This couldn't be more perfect of an evening," she continued sarcastically.

With a shrug, Brett went halfway down the creaky wooden steps and sat. "I agree," he said.

Kelly's eyes flicked over to him. He had a thoughtful look on his face. Even though she hadn't seen it for a few years, she knew what it meant. Something was on his mind. However, she wasn't the least bit interested in finding out what it was. There was only one thing she wanted—out of the basement.

Her nose tickled from the typical basement must, and she wished she'd taken an allergy pill. Too late now.

Opening the box she had carried earlier, she rooted through it, looking for anything to take the door down.

"It's not going to work," Brett told her.

"What's not?" she asked, closing the box and moving to another.

"Taking the door off the hinges." Brett got up and came down the stairs.

"Why not?" Kelly asked, wondering how he knew what she was thinking. "It works in the movies."

"Sure," Brett agreed. "But the hinges are the wrong way. However," he looked back at the door thoughtfully, "maybe we could take the doorknob off. That would give us a hole to yell through."

"Great," Kelly said. "It's a start. Maybe we can find something to take out those screws. Doesn't have to be a screwdriver. Scissors might work. If we are careful, we don't strip the screws."

She felt Brett moving closer, and stepped, putting a small stack of boxes between them.

"Hey," Brett said.

Something in his tone made her look up at him. "What?"

Brett crossed his arms. "Why did you break up with me?"

Kelly stared back at him, her jaw dropping open slightly. He wanted to talk about this *now*?

Chapter 6

The words came out of Brett's lips before he'd even realized it. When Kelly froze, her hands buried deep inside a box of random junk, it made him curious. He knew it had something to do with Megan all those years go, but since Kelly hadn't bothered to return his texts, calls, or emails, now was as good of a time as any to find out why.

And she couldn't run. The basement was only so big.

Carefully, as though the cardboard were some precious, expensive thing, she resealed the box and rested her hands on top of it before looking at him. Kelly stared at him for a full minute, making him feel nervous under her sharp gaze. Finally, she answered.

"I'm pretty sure you know why."

The glare coming off of her was so intense, he laughed and threw up his hands. "Ouch." When she didn't budge, he shook his head. "Actually, I don't."

"No guesses at all?" Kelly asked. She put her hands on her hips.

It was a pose Brett remembered from when they were together. It was her challenging pose. The one she gave when she was about to go off on someone. Her eyes were sparking, and not in a good way.

He didn't answer. When she was like this, nothing would calm her.

When she realized he wasn't going to say anything, Kelly crossed her arms. "Two words. Megan Hollister."

Brett nodded. He knocked on a box, and when it felt sturdy enough, sat on it. "I know Megan. What about her?"

Kelly huffed. It was adorable. Even after several years of adulthood, she still acted the same. He couldn't help it when he smiled. He'd missed her attitude. Even though it was obvious she wasn't interested in him anymore, he was glad to have a little closure. Getting locked in a basement wasn't his idea of fun, but hey, it might work out well.

"I saw the two of you," she said slowly, seeming to search for the words she wanted to say, "the night before I left for college. When you were supposed to be with me, you were with her. Holding her tightly. Smiling at her."

She bit her lip and looked down. When she looked back up, there was something in her eyes he couldn't quite make out. They were sad. Hurt. Angry. All mixed together.

"What you saw—"

"No. I don't want to hear an excuse."

Brett shrugged. "Good. Because I don't have one."

Kelly's head snapped up and she looked at him. "So you admit it? You and Megan were..."

"I can't tell you what happened," Brett told her. "It isn't my story. Megan was going through a hard time. She was actually looking for you, but couldn't find you. I was there. Right place, right time, to help her. She begged me not to tell anyone. Turns out for me, though, for us," he motioned between the two of them, "it was the wrong place, wrong time."

Kelly didn't answer. Her eyes were narrowed.

"I know you don't like that answer," Brett said. "But it's the truth. Ask her yourself."

"No thanks," Kelly said, and she turned, starting to poke through another box. "I'm done with this conversation, with Megan, and with you."

"I'm not," Brett said. "And we are stuck here together, so let's have at it. Work through it. Either mend our fence or burn our bridge, but let's just get it out and move on, whichever way we are supposed to."

Kelly turned to face him. "Why is that so important to you?" she asked. The crossed her arms, ready to hear whatever excuse he had this time. She jutted her chin out, and gave him her most challenging stairs.

But then he surprised her. Brett shrugged, shook his head, and met her eyes.

"Because I love you. Even now."

Chapter 7

Love. Brett was claiming to love her. But that look he'd had for Megan... Kelly shook her head. This whole conversation was upsetting. It was bringing back up memories she didn't like. Memories of her and Brett laughing together, smiling, kissing. Memories her him with someone else in his arms, holding her close.

She felt a little sick to her stomach. It was likely the musty smell in the basement. She felt a little dizzy and longed for fresh air. To be out of the basement and away from Brett.

His words seemed to float on the air, circling around and around in her mind like a Ferris wheel.

Love.

It was confusing her. Maybe she should listen to what he had to say. Brett was right. They were trapped here. Maybe this was a chance for closure, one way or another. The idea didn't sound bad. Maybe that was something that she needed as well.

They had known each other a long time. Maybe...just maybe, she owed him a chance to explain himself. It didn't mean she had to accept whatever excuse he gave, but she could at least let him talk. What was the harm?

Kelly looked away for a moment, then stalked over to the stairs and sat, her feet resting on the floor. "Fine. Talk."

Brett sighed. "You're always like this," he said. His words were almost a snarl.

"Like what?" She crossed her arms.

"Defensive. Jumping to conclusions."

He didn't say it unkindly, but it still made Kelly grind her teeth. *She* was the victim here. It was *her* boyfriend who had been...whatever it was with Megan.

"Maybe that's because you do stupid stuff," she snapped. If he wanted to have an attitude, she'd match it.

"Stupid stuff? Like what?" Now it was Brett's turn to cross his arms.

"Like have your arms around another girl."

Brett let out a growl of frustration. "It was a hug, Kelly. Like you gave to plenty of our friends. Even the guys. Especially the guys."

Kelly opened her mouth to argue, and then stopped. He was right. She'd given plenty of hugs over the years. And to guys. Brett never got upset at her for that. Maybe she'd overreacted a little. After all, she still didn't know what Brett and Megan had been talking about.

She closed her eyes for a moment, willing her memory to recall that evening. Was it possible that she had jumped to conclusions and the last several years of heartache and anger had been without a good reason? She'd actually never considered that before now. Or the fact of how Brett might have felt, with her suddenly storming off and not speaking to him again.

For years.

If that had happened to her, she'd be devastated. She nodded slowly, while she chewed her lip.

Okay. I can give him this. I can listen to his side.

Brett spoke, and as he did, her mind replayed that evening. "I was looking for you. I was coming back from washing up. Remember how Tyson Bailey spilled his punch on my shirt?"

She nodded and met his eyes.

"Megan was coming out of the ladies room. She'd been crying. I asked if she was okay, and she asked if I knew where you were. I told her probably in the room with the refreshments. She nodded, and started to go there."

He stopped, then his eyes clouded. "Not five seconds later, her phone pinged, she looked at it, burst out crying, and fell into my arms. That's when you walked around the corner and saw us."

"Then why didn't she say anything?" Kelly asked. "Why didn't you?"

"You didn't give me a chance to," Brett said quietly. "And Megan, she never ever saw you. She ran back into the ladies room. Remember?"

Kelly thought back to that moment. At the time, she'd thought Megan ran from her. But it was true. Megan had never seen her. She hadn't turned, she'd just run. And then Kelly had gotten angry. She'd yelled, then punched Brett, and ran away herself.

A phantom pain appeared in her knuckles at the memory. Her mouth felt dry. It was hot and stuffy in the basement, and her throat still itched from the slightly musty smell. She wished there was something to drink.

And a way to avoid what she knew she needed to say next. Brett sat on the box, just watching her. There wasn't any anger in his face, just hurt. That...that was difficult to see, especially knowing that she'd put that hurt there.

"I'm sorry," Kelly said. She meant it too, and admitted, "You are right. I've always been quick to get upset. I think I've gotten better over the years. But I still jump to conclusions." She toyed with her watch, running a finger over the band.

"I just wish you'd given me a chance to explain," Brett said. His eyes were sorrowful. "Kelly, we don't have to pick up where we left off, but can't we at least be friends again? It would make things less awkward at times like this."

There was a pause, and then Brett rubbed at his jaw. "Besides, I'd like to know how you are doing. If you get that agent position at the realtor. If you," he stopped, then seemed to visibly push himself on, "if you find someone. Get married. Have kids."

Kelly realized her hands were trembling. Hearing Brett say that made her realize something. It wasn't someone else she wanted those things with. It was him. It had always been him.

Chapter 8

Brett watched Kelly. He could tell she was considering his words. He could also tell that she wanted to say something, but wasn't letting herself.

Suppressing a sigh, Brett stood and walked over to the stairs. "I'm going to look at the door again," he said. He knew there was tension in his voice, but he didn't care. There he'd just poured his heart out, and Kelly didn't want to say anything.

She nodded and moved to let him past. Brett jiggled at the door handle, wondering if he took off the knob if it would let him have access to remove the door.

He'd bent over to inspect the screw type when there was a click, and the door opened. He pitched forward and quickly righted himself from the stumble.

"Kids?"

Relief filled him. Kelly sprang up and pushed past him, nearly knocking him down the stairs. "Daddy! Thank goodness," she said, wrapping her arms around her dad.

"Good thing I came back," her dad grinned. "I wanted to get a different pot for my flower. Mildred is using a black one. I thought white might make my flowers pop better. When I saw almost none of the boxes moved, I had a feeling the door got you."

"Sure did," Brett said. He eyed the door. "Mind if I just take it off the hinges for a while so we don't have this happen again?"

"As long as you put it back, be my guest," Kelly's dad said. "I'm heading back to the fair. It's hands off the plants in an hour. Want to make sure mine looks her best. You two be good."

Brett nodded, already tugging the pins out of the hinges. He couldn't hear what Kelly said to her dad as she walked away, stepping outside with him, but a moment later, she was back carrying a box.

Wordlessly, the two of them carried the boxes from the garage down the steps and stacked them, returned to the garage, and then repeated the action. With the door removed, there was no chance of them getting locked in again, but he saw Kelly bring her phone downstairs and set it on a shelf.

"Good idea," he commented.

She didn't answer.

They worked for nearly two hours, and his legs were starting to ache. He wondered if Kelly felt the same, but she didn't complain, and she didn't talk much. Just an occasional "excuse me" when they nearly bumped. That way okay, though. He could tell she was thinking, by the range of emotions flickering across her face.

Hopefully, she was thinking about what he'd said about at least being friends.

Little by little, the pile of boxes to carry dwindled. As Kelly grabbed the last one to carry down, Brett replaced the basement door on its hinges and stepped outside to guzzle a bottle of water.

Dusk was approaching, and Brett put a hand on his back and stretched as he stared up into the sky. A sunset in Pumpkin City was always a sight to behold. The colors were vibrant—scarlet bleeding into violet to a navy blue before vanishing into darkness. Today, a few clouds swept across the sky, creating colorful shapes.

"That one looks like the Ferris wheel at the fair," Kelly said, standing at his elbow.

Brett startled. He hadn't heard her come up from the basement. "Yeah," he said.

They were quiet for a moment, then she asked, "I'm going to see my dad's flower there tomorrow. Are you going too?"

"I might," Brett said. He looked over at her. "Want to go with me?"

Kelly sucked in an audible breath, but she nodded, and a second later offered up a smile. It seemed genuine. "Sure. Pick me up at four?"

"Sounds good," he answered. Before she could change her mind, he added, "I'll see you then. Right now, I'm going to go shower and get some pain killer in me before the stiffness sets in. Some of those boxes just about did me in."

Kelly laughed. "Old man."

"And proud of it," Brett said. "It's a privilege not afforded to all!" He waved and jogged back to his parents' house. As he hit his second shower of the day, he wondered, was Kelly's agreeing to go to the fair a peace offering? She really hadn't said, and their conversation in the basement hadn't really wrapped up.

There wasn't that sense of closure or of a new beginning. Toweling off, he frowned at his reflection and asked, "What happens next?"

Chapter 9

Kelly couldn't believe she'd agreed to go with Brett. It had just sort of slipped out. For a moment, as they'd been staring at the clouds, she'd forgotten. It was like time hadn't passed at all. Things were comfortable, friendly, and how they used to be.

She bit her lip as she stared into the mirror. For some reason, she felt a little nervous. But why? Tugging her jeans up a little higher, and smoothing her button up casual blouse, she looked at herself critically.

Which, she didn't know why she was doing. It wasn't like this was a date. Not really.

She was back home, and seeing all the people she'd grown up around, so she didn't want to look like a total slob. Yeah. That was all. This wasn't about Brett. Not one bit.

And if she told herself that enough times, maybe she'd start to believe it.

Kelly threw her hair into a ponytail and pulled on a pair of sneakers. It was hot out, and a little muggy feeling, and sandals would be a nicer looking and not feel as stifling, but chances were there would be some horse droppings in the field where the fair was, and if she stepped on one, she didn't want it squishing between her toes.

She laughed, and realized that something like that was commonplace to Pumpkin City, but in the city where she worked, they'd never believe it could happen. There, no one drove around in a wagon with a horse pulling it. Here, at least half of the town's population got around that way, not by car.

The doorbell rang, and Kelly ran down the stairs. This evening, she determined, would be one of fresh starts. She'd thought about it all day. The plan was to act like nothing had happened and enjoy her weekend home. She always had looked forward to the fair, and she'd missed it the last few years, refusing to come home in case she ran into Brett.

But finally, the worst had happened...and it really wasn't as bad as she'd been worrying about. She and Brett were older now. More mature. They could work out their problems like grownups. And they had, sort of. Even if she hadn't said much in reply, or anything at all, after his offer of friendship.

Kelly grabbed her purse, making sure she had a house key. Her parents had left an hour before. Her dad didn't want to risk anything happening to his plant. Someone had recently moved in down the street and had also entered a flower, he'd said last night, and he was worried about sabotage. She'd have giggled except for the concerned expression on his face. Evidently, her father and Mildred had planned not to leave their flowers alone today until the judging happened.

Opening the door, Kelly looked in surprise. Instead of Brett's white truck, there was a chestnut horse attached to a small wagon. "Going green with our ride?" she asked.

"Well, greener," Brett answered. "You know Mr. Mason down the street a ways?" At her nod, he continued, "He asked if I could take this wagon he'd repaired back to the owner at the fair. He's working the funnel cakes. I figured we can catch a ride or else walk back. It's not too far really, and the weather is good."

"Sure," Kelly said, and locked the front door behind her. She climbed onto the narrow bench seat and held on to the wagon's side as Brett flicked the reins.

"Walk on," he called to the horse.

As they moved forward, the wagon's wheels bouncing along the graveled road, Brett grinned at Kelly. "Remember the hay ride in fourth grade? I don't know why, but this suddenly made me think of it."

Kelly's eyes got big. "I do," she said, as the memory hit her. "We'd all climbed in the back, but then Marcie dropped her shoe and the driver got down to get it."

"Right." Brett took up the story. "When the driver climbed out to get it, that troublemaker Josh climbed in the seat and smacked the horses, making them take off."

Kelly shuddered. "That was scary. I've never seen our teacher move so fast. She just about vaulted from the wagon's back to the seat, grabbed the reins, and stopped the horses."

"Scariest moment in my life, just about," Brett mused.

"I'll bet it was scarier for Josh," Kelly laughed. "I understood his dad punished him pretty good." She sat up suddenly, and pointed, "I see it!"

It didn't matter how many times she'd been to the summer fair. Each time, Kelly felt like a little girl. It wasn't but a moment later that the smells of the fair—corn dogs, freshly made cotton candy, and funnel cakes—hit her nose. The sound of people laughing, children and teens screaming on rides, and a muffled sounding voice over a loudspeaker filled her ears.

"Sit down," Brett warned, and Kelly realized she was half standing in the wagon. Plopping back down, she waited impatiently for him to park with the other horses.

Jumping out, she hitched the horse while Brett set the brake. "Where to first?" she asked. "Dinner or tickets? Or do you need to let the horse's owner know?"

"Dinner," Brett said. "I sure don't want to miss out on the food. I'll find the guy in a bit, but he already knows I was bringing his horse and wagon."

Kelly didn't disagree. After a few moments of surveying their options, she went for freshly breaded fried chicken fingers and onion rings sold by the fire department, while

Brett got a foot-long chili dog sold by the local youth group.

"Let's get some drinks, then sit," Brett said, pointing to a large booth marked with drink choices.

Nodding, Kelly followed him past the cake walk, where homemade cakes and pies, many of them Amish made, crowded a large stand for winners to choose from.

It seemed as if the whole town was here. Children and teenagers, Amish and not, walked around with smiles, while their parents stood in small groups socializing.

Her head twisted to the side to see what games were available and she bumped right into someone. Managing to keep her food in the little cardboard tray, she looked up to apologize when she saw who it was.

Megan Hollister.

Chapter 10

Sidestepping quickly, Brett managed to protect his dinner from three children who bolted past. He looked over his shoulder to see if Kelly was okay, but Kelly wasn't following. She'd stopped and was staring at another woman. All at once, his shoulders tensed. It was Megan.

Just when things were going well.

Brett walked back and gave a half wave. "Hey," he said.

Megan glanced between the two of them and broke into a huge smile. "Wow! It's so good to see both of you, and together, too! Are you guys dating again?"

He could tell Kelly felt uncomfortable. "Um," she said, "No. Just here as friends."

"Friends is a start," Megan said. Then she bit her lip. "I've been a crummy friend, Kelly. It's good to see you here. I want to apologize to you."

Brett's eyes flicked to Kelly. Her eyes had widened, and she looked surprised.

"What do you mean?" Kelly asked.

"I mean—" Megan shook her head. "You've got your hands full. Here, let's go to a table. I was about to eat myself," she motioned to the chicken sandwich in her hand. "How about that table over there?"

Brett nodded. "Good idea. How about some drinks? I'll go grab them."

"Lemonade," Kelly said, at the same time Megan requested a Diet Coke.

"Gotcha. Back in a few," he said.

Setting his hotdog down, he headed to the closest drink booth. He didn't want to be gone long in case things got out of hand. He knew from experience Kelly wasn't one to back down from a confrontation, and Megan, captain of the debate team, had been very good at arguing too.

Worry over what might be going on led him to drum his fingers against his thigh as he waited in the line. He resisted taking more than a few glances over his shoulder. So far, so good. He hoped it would stay that way.

The line moved agonizingly slow. Brett finally approached the counter, requested the three drinks, and placed his cash down. Then he waited some more. It was a family stand staffed by children at the front, and the adults filling the orders, so first the little girl had to repeat his order a few times before she got it right. Then she had to count out his money, and then his change. Finally, he got the drinks and spun around, weaving his way between the fair goers toward the table he'd left Kelly and Megan.

He approached just in time to hear Kelly shout, "I don't believe you."

Oh great.

Chapter 11

When Brett left, Kelly sat and squirted ketchup from a packet onto the side of her cardboard tray. Megan sat silently, poking at her sandwich. Finally, she looked up. "I'm sorry."

"You said that earlier," Kelly said. "And you should be. Trying to steal my boyfriend? You didn't want us together, and you succeeded. Congrats." She glared, but it was directed at an onion ring.

"Steal Brett? What do you mean?"

The surprise in Megan's voice made Kelly look up. She frowned. "Don't act like you don't know."

Megan shook her head slowly. "But I don't, Kelly. Really."

"So you don't remember the huge party we all had the night before we left for college?"

Megan's eyes filled with tears. "I do. That's why I want to apologize. I never said goodbye. I...I have been a crummy friend, avoiding you for four years."

"So you admit it." Kelly set down her chicken finger. "You were trying to steal Brett from me. One last try to get him, huh?"

"I wouldn't!" Megan protested. "I promise."

"Then what happened?" Kelly asked. "Why were you two holding each other?"

Megan frowned. "I don't remember that," she said.

"I do," Kelly said. "I came around the corner, near the restrooms, and you were holding on to Brett. Then, you suddenly pulled away and ran into the ladies room."

"Ohhh." Megan was quiet a moment and nodded slowly. "I remember that. I didn't know you were there, though."

"I don't believe you," Kelly said, half standing. Her voice must have been loud, because several people looked over.

Brett came rushing up and set the drinks down. "Everything okay?" he asked.

"There's been a misunderstanding," Megan said. She held out her hands in a pleading gesture.

"Maybe you'd better start talking then," Kelly said. She saw Brett open his mouth and glared at him. "Her. Not you. I was just starting to like you again."

Brett waved a napkin as though it were a white flag, then picked up his foot long and took a bite.

"Kelly, I don't know what you saw, or what you think you saw, but it wasn't me trying to steal Brett," Megan said. "I guess it makes sense now though. I wondered why I never saw pictures of you two on Facebook."

Closing her eyes for a moment, Kelly huffed out a breath and counted to ten slowly. This weekend was too full of the past. Too full of old friends. It was like the universe was pushing her together with these people and memories she didn't want. But it must be for a reason, so she took another breath, let it out slowly, and said, "Okay. Tell me then. Why did you vanish for four years? You didn't reach out, try to apologize, say hello, nothing. Why?"

Megan looked down at her sandwich. Her long, light brown hair nearly covered her face. It took a moment, but finally she looked up, and her eyes were sorrowful.

"Because I avoided you, and just about everyone else I knew because I was so humiliated."

"But why? Humiliated about what?" Kelly asked, genuinely curious. Here, she thought she'd been the one avoiding everyone. Why did Megan think it was her?

"It's really stupid now," Megan admitted. "But that night at the party, it was a total bragfest. Everyone was talking about where they were going, what they were doing…everyone seemed to have their plans and their lives all planned and perfect."

She stopped and looked at Kelly, but Kelly had just shoved in half a chicken finger and was eying her dwindling ketchup supply. Running a finger on a drop of condensation outside of her Diet Coke, Megan continued, "Well, we were all dancing, having fun, when I got a call from my mom. I excused myself and went where it was quieter. Long story short, that scholarship I'd gotten? They'd made a mistake. Megan Hollister *had* won the scholarship," she broke off and pointed to herself with an angry look, "but not this Megan. It was someone else. With my name."

Kelly's mouth dropped. "Are you serious? And they waited that long to tell you? The night before?"

"Yeah." Megan looked down again.

Kelly could tell that even years later the memory hurt her friend. She wished she could do something. Had known. But she'd cut everyone off because of her anger. The same way Megan had, because of her embarrassment. Now it was Kelly's turn to feel like a crummy friend.

"Why didn't you tell me?" Kelly asked, her voice soft. "We were best friends. I could have...I don't know, but I could have maybe made you feel better. Somehow."

"Because!" Megan waved a hand around, "You, the golden girl, were off to a great school. Everyone was, or else headed to a great job. Me? Well, now I didn't know what I was going to do. When I found out I'd never even gotten the scholarship, that it was a clerical error, do you know how I felt?" Her voice was filled with frustration. "You know my folks don't have money. This scholarship meant the world to us. It meant a generational change, even. The first in the family to go to college. The last thing I wanted to do was to see anyone and have them find out. I didn't want pity. I wanted to be like everyone else—my life put together."

"You told Brett though," Kelly said, unable to keep the accusation out of her voice.

"I didn't want to," Megan said. "But I'm glad I did. He...made me feel better. He told me that my worth wasn't tied to a school or a scholarship. That I'd find something better. It took me a long time to realize he was right."

Kelly traced her finger on the table. "So, what did you do then? Did you go to school somewhere else?"

"I did," Megan said. "I went to the community college. Night classes, since I worked during the day. I managed to get myself a two-year degree, and I'm working, slowly, toward a nursing degree. I have a job at the nursing home. They are pretty good about working around my classes. You know me, always got to work." She flashed a smile.

A surge of guilt washed through Kelly. It was true. Megan always had to. It wasn't because she wanted to, but because her family needed her to. Megan didn't seem too upset anymore, but it must have been so hard for her at first. And she'd had to do it all on her own.

Megan took a deep breath and looked Kelly right in the eyes. "I'm glad we got to see each other again. I want to know...are we still friends? Can you forgive me?"

Chapter 12

His foot long down to just a few bites, Brett reached for his drink. He couldn't eat much slower to pretend he wasn't listening, but he didn't want to miss Kelly's answer by standing up and getting something else.

Kelly and Megan had been friends almost as long as the two of them had been, when Megan moved in to their third-grade classroom.

Looking over the rim of his bottle of water, he couldn't help but stare. Megan was looking at Kelly with a pleading expression. Kelly had a thoughtful expression on her face, and her hands in her lap. Finally, she spoke.

"You know, it sounds like it was all a misunderstanding. Kind of like I had with Brett. And you know what else?"

Kelly was quiet for so long, Brett was feeling just as nervous looking as Megan. Finally, she finished, "I realize that I've wasted a lot of time being upset and maybe I was in part to blame for us not talking for so long. I thought you had betrayed me. Really, what I should have done was said something to you that night. Then we'd wouldn't have ignored each other."

"I'm really glad you said that," Megan said, and her tense looking shoulders lowered. "I wasted a lot of time too, being too proud and embarrassed. I'm ashamed that I didn't trust you enough to support me."

"I would have, and I will," Kelly promised. "From now on, if I've a problem with anyone, I'm going to talk with them about it, not assume anything. And I want you to call me if you need me. Maybe I can help somehow."

"I'm glad to hear that," Brett said. Both women looked at him like they'd forgotten he was there and he shrugged. "What?"

Megan laughed and stood up, grabbing her sandwich. "I've got to leave to make it to work in time. Text me," she said, taking Kelly's phone and punching in her number. "Let's get together soon."

Kelly nodded and waved. When Megan was out of sight, she turned to Brett. "You should have told me," she said. "Why didn't you? You let me think the worst all these years." Her tone was accusing.

"No, I didn't," Brett said. "That was all you. You never gave me a chance to say anything. Not even to explain that you needed to hear it from Megan herself, until yesterday."

Kelly sighed. He was right. She dropped her head into her hands. "I really am the worst."

"Nah," Brett said. "Just impulsive, competitive, strong willed, thick headed—"

"Geez! Enough," Kelly said, throwing a crumpled napkin at him.

"I'm not done," he said, and starting ticking off on his fingers, "Beautiful, funny, clever—"

This time he was interrupted, as Kelly leaned in, her lips alarmingly close to his.

Chapter 13

Brett's eyes were so close to hers, she couldn't even see anything else. She didn't know what had made her move in so closely, but just as quickly she backed away and scrambled up.

Frozen for a moment, they just stared at each other, neither speaking. "Uh," Brett cleared his throat, "want to walk around?"

"Sure." Kelly grabbed her trash and dropped it in a nearby barrel. Her heart was beating quickly. What had almost happened? Had she been about to hug him? Kiss him? She wasn't sure. Her body had reacted before her mind had. It was almost subconscious.

What was more frustrating was that she wouldn't have minded it, but what about Brett? There was still distance between them. They were friendly, but were they still friends? Had the time passed that they could be more? Kelly didn't want to assume anything. She knew it was all because of her, too.

In the last twenty-four hours, she'd realized just how much time she'd wasted, both with Brett and with Megan. How much had she missed out on because of her reaction to that night?

Worse still, she'd hurt those she cared about. She hadn't been there for Megan when her dreams had been dashed because of a clerical error. Megan's family was probably counting on that scholarship. Her dad was a farmer and her mom a seamstress. They never had a lot of extra money, which is why Megan had worked a job after school when she was sixteen. To have gotten a full scholarship and have it yanked away must have been painful for the whole family.

And what about Brett? How many things had he needed someone for, and she hadn't been there?

"You look like you're thinking pretty hard," Brett said as they walked slowly around the field.

Paused in front of a game booth, Kelly watched teenagers trying to pop a balloon with a dart. There were cheers as the dart flew perfectly, then groans as it bounced off the balloon.

"Those things are always rigged," she commented.

"Never stopped me from trying," Brett laughed. "Must have spent fifty bucks on that thing one year, trying to win you a huge teddy bear."

"I liked the fish much better," Kelly assured him, thinking about the goldfish he'd won later at a different game with his last dollar.

"Yeah, Goldie was pretty cool, wasn't she?" he said. "But you didn't tell me what you were thinking about."

Kelly started walking again. "I don't know. A lot. Maybe I'm growing up. I've realized that maybe I am a little too impulsive. Quick to get angry. Slow to forgive."

With a shrug, Brett said, "It happens. We can all get that way."

"Not you." Kell almost said it sadly. "You don't ever. Things happen and you shrug and just keep going."

"What else am I supposed to do?" Brett asked her mildly. He stopped in front of a ring toss game, watched for a moment, then walked on. "Moping or getting upset doesn't do anything. Things happen, and when they do, we just have to find a way to keep going. I have too much to do to just let life pass me by because I was upset."

Kelly frowned. That sounded like what she'd been doing.

"Of course," he continued, and stopped to meet her eyes, "that doesn't mean things happen that don't hurt me. Make me want to curl up in a ball. But after a while, after years of trying to get hold of someone, you just figure you have to..." his voice grew softer, "let them go because they don't want you."

"And if they wanted you again?" Kelly asked. "If they never had stopped wanting you?"

A child holding a balloon rushed past, chased by two others. One bumped into Kelly, knocking her forward into Brett.

He reached out and steadied her, his hands on her elbows. Brett looked down at her, and his warm eyes and smile made her feel tingly and breathless.

"Well then," he whispered, close in her ear, "She'd have to tell me that."

Was it that simple? Could it be? Kelly swallowed. Brett's arms wrapped around her and she breathed in deeply. For a moment, she let her eyes close and rested her head against his chest.

She'd missed this. Missed Brett. But a tiny nagging feeling was in the back of her head.

If she did tell him she missed him, wanted him still, and apologized, if she asked for a second chance...would he give it to her?

Chapter 14

With Kelly in his arms, Brett was fighting himself not to tip his head down and kiss her hair. He inhaled her strawberry scent and closed his eyes briefly.

Reluctantly stepping back, he smiled at her. "I'm going to grab some tickets," he said.

"Umm yeah, I'm still thirsty. I'll grab us some lemonade," she said, turning away as he walked the few steps to the nearby booth.

His eyes were focused on the person in front of him as he waited for his turn. Brett shuffled forward and when someone grabbed his arm he didn't notice at first, thinking it was Kelly. He looked over with a smile, then his eyebrows raised. "Wendy."

"That's right!" Wendy, the head cheerleader when they were in high school, and the girl who'd been chasing after him with Facebook messages and texts for the last few years, smiled up at him. Tiny and cute, she'd always been a favorite of the guys, which was why Brett wasn't interested. He preferred a girl who wasn't after every guy on every team.

"Hey," he said, trying to free his arm.

"Here alone?" she asked, holding on tighter. "Maybe we could go on some rides together. There's a dark ride," she said suggestively, and giggled up at him.

"Thanks, but I'm—"

"Got our drinks," Kelly said, interrupting at just the right time. Her eyes took in Wendy, her arms wrapped around Brett's arm, and the perfectly practiced pout Wendy still had, even after all these years.

"Oh. Are you two back together?" Wendy asked, her disappointment evident.

"Next!" the man selling tickets waved to them.

Brett stepped forward. "Two wristbands," he said, handing over some cash.

When he turned back, Wendy was gone. "Looking for your girlfriend?" Kelly asked, raising her eyebrows.

"Nope," Brett said, handing Kelly one of the wristbands. He put his on, helped her with hers, and answered, "Don't have one anymore, remember?"

Kelly didn't answer, but her face flushed. It could have been the heat, even with the sun starting to dip it was hot, but he didn't think so.

Brett drank deeply from the cup of lemonade she'd handed him. "Thanks. This really hits the spot," he said.

"One day, I'm going to buy one of those machines and make my own fresh lemonade any time I want it," Kelly agreed.

"Invite me over when you do," Brett said. And then he stopped. It had come out so casual. Too casual. For a moment, he'd forgotten that they weren't together, because being with her felt so natural.

To his immense relief, she said, "Yeah, sure." Then Kelly pointed. "How about that one?"

Brett looked at the spinning monstrosity in front of him. Visions of his foot-long danced before him, but he nodded and smiled, hoping his dinner wouldn't make a second appearance after—or worse, during—the ride she wanted. "Sure," he said, a little weakly.

Kelly didn't seem to notice. She led him to the line. Before he knew it, he was strapped into a giant circle, trapped with screaming children and adults. It took all of his efforts to make sure his dinner didn't reemerge. Kelly didn't seem to be having that problem though. She laughed and threw her hands into the air, and grinned widely at him when the ride was over.

Brett couldn't stop the matching grin on his face. He'd forgotten how big of a kid Kelly was when it came to rides. It didn't matter what it was, she enjoyed every second of it.

They rode the carousel next. It wasn't a huge one, only two horses across, but Kelly raced him to the horses, and climbed on the one with a bright red saddle. As the music played and they started to spin, she called, "My horse is faster than yours!"

It made him laugh, and he pretended to race her. When the ride was over, she pointed in the distance and dragged him on one ride after the next. Thankfully, a few were calm, and allowed his churning stomach a chance to catch up after all the spinning.

The sun dipped lower and lower, and soon the night was lit from the booths and the ride's neon colors. Over in one tent, Bingo was being called, while the music for the cake walk trickled past as they passed another.

"I'm having a great time," Kelly said. "Thanks for taking me."

She smiled at him, but Brett wasn't sure what kind of a smile it was. This whole evening had been confusing, and he hoped that he figured it out soon. Were they friends? More? Was she wanting to pick up where they'd left off? He was anxious to know, but at the same time too worried to ask.

"Glad you came with me," he answered instead. *There, that was neutral.*

They strolled to the large Ferris wheel. Couples of all ages were in the seats, some giggling and screaming or waving to friends below. Others were kissing each other, or cuddled close.

As they got in the long line that snaked around the dunking booth, where a person in a swimsuit was teasing the throwers, and a scouting group selling candy apples, Brett couldn't help but grin. He and Kelly had their first kiss here, when they were seventeen. He wondered if she remembered.

A quick glance over at her showed the hint of a smile, and he could tell she did.

Suddenly, Brett wondered, what if he tried to kiss her tonight? Would she let him? Or would she try to break his nose again?

Chapter 15

The line moved so slowly. It was three full rides before it was their turn to climb on the Ferris wheel. A quick glance at her watch showed it was nearing ten, and the fair would end after the fireworks at half past.

"Yes! Got the blue," Brett crowed, as he lowered the safety bar and stuck in the locking piece.

Kelly just shook her head but didn't answer. She knew that was his favorite, but really, they were all the same. Weren't they?

As they settled in, the car moving so the next couple could ride, she shifted to get more comfortable.

"Hey look!" Brett said. "We've been in this bucket before!" He pointed to a worn-looking heart with a B and a K etched in.

"Oh my gosh. We have. Wow, it's been what...five years? Six, since we did that?" Kelly asked in amazement. "How crazy It's the same ride!"

"Yeah," Brett answered. They moved up again while another couple climbed in. "All kinds of things from the past today."

"Mmm." Kelly didn't say anything else. She wasn't sure if she should. Things were going well. Why mess it up? There was a little part of her that was glad, maybe even a little smug, that he'd seen Wendy and turned her down. No one had ever turned Wendy down. I mean, if the head cheerleader was interested in you, what guy wouldn't be?

But then, she remembered. Brett. That's who. He'd never been interested in Wendy. He'd only ever had eyes for her.

A warm feeling came over her then, and she shyly looked at Brett. He caught her eyes and reached for her hand to squeeze it. His touch felt comfortable. Familiar. Like something she'd missed. She squeezed his hand back.

Slowly, slowly, they finally filled the ride, and the wheel moved in earnest.

"Wheeee!" Kelly squealed as they circled.

"It's going fast," Brett called, over the shrieks of the two girls above them.

"It really is!" Kelly said. "Hey, let's get some popcorn next."

They spun around another full rotation, nearing the top. Brett opened his mouth to answer when there was a loud cracking sound, and the Ferris wheel jolted, coming to a sudden stop.

The ride cars swung wildly, and the screams that had been excited sounding just a moment before were now terrified.

Kelly looked down and regretted that decision instantly. The ride operator was gesturing wildly. He looked frantic and had pulled out a phone. Her stomach clenched, and she was not sure she wanted to know what was happening.

When she leaned back, Brett's arm wrapped around her. "We're fine," he assured her. "I'm sure it will start up soon and let us off."

Kelly nodded, but any words she might have had were caught in her throat. Something was really wrong, she was sure of it, and she was scared. Her eyes darted to Brett. He looked calm, but there was the telltale tightness in his eyes, which indicated he was also a little nervous.

"Hey, you know, couldn't be a better place for this to happen," he joked, and pointed off in the distance.

Kelly followed his finger and laughed. He was right. The firefighters had abandoned their food and game booth, and were pushing toward the stuck ride. "Very true," she answered.

They sat in silence. Most everyone did. There were a few sniffles from somewhere, but most everyone sat and talked quietly or not at all.

Brett finally broke the silence. "You know," he said, "it kind of feels like the universe keeps pushing us together."

Kelly thought about it for a moment, then nodded. She had thought the same earlier. "You might be right."

They were quiet again, listening as a man spoke through the fair's sound system. "Stay in your seat. Do not move. We will rescue you, but you need to hold still. A part has broken and so we are going to bring you in manually."

"A part is broken?" Kelly squeaked. "Oh my gosh! Are we going to fall?" Her chest felt tight.

"Don't worry," Brett said. "I think it was just the motor. That's why they are going to bring us in slowly. If it was anything serious, they'd have the firemen take us down on the ladder."

Kelly thought about that a moment. He was likely right. That made her feel better. "I wonder how long it will take," she said, slightly regretting all the lemonade she'd had to drink.

Brett leaned over slightly and the seat tipped. Kelly shrieked and grabbed the side. "Don't do that," she gasped. "I don't want to fall!"

"Sorry," he said, straightening. "No idea." He leaned back in his seat, staring up at the sky. "Good view for the fireworks though."

"Yeah," Kelly answered. "That's true." She appreciated his effort at small talk, but was anxious to get down. Hopefully, it would be soon.

"So, you aren't seeing anyone right now?" she asked.

Where did that come from? Brett looked as surprised as she felt. She wondered why that had popped out of her mouth.

"Not right now," he said. "Had my heart broken once. Not ready for it again."

Kelly bit her lip. Of course not. Why did the idea of them getting back together even cross her mind? She'd been stupid, and Brett was forgiving and laid back, but he also wasn't going to want to get back in a relationship so easily. Especially with her.

That was her fault, and she was paying the price for it.

There was a grinding sound as the ride lurched forward then stopped. Shouts came from below. Kelly dared a quick peek then leaned back again.

"How's it look?" Brett asked.

"I have no idea what I'm looking for," Kelly admitted. "But there are a lot of people crowded around down there."

"Good. Softer landing if we crash," Brett said.

Kelly's mouth opened as she gaped at him. Then she laughed. He winked at her and pulled her close. The night air had shifted almost suddenly. It had gone from being muggy in the line to much cooler.

"Warm enough?" he asked.

"With you here I am," she answered, and leaned into his shoulder. When he didn't say anything or pull away, she looked up at him. Once she'd summoned her courage, she would ask.

"Brett," Kelly whispered finally. "Do you believe in second chances?"

Chapter 16

Being this close to Kelly was driving him crazy. She fit so well under his shoulder. He wasn't in a hurry for the ride to work again. Earlier, when he'd joked about the universe pushing them together, he was only half joking.

What would happen if he just leaned over and kissed her? Brett considered the idea, then with his free hand rubbed his nose that had suddenly started tingling. He didn't want it punched.

With a sigh, he looked at his watch. They'd been trapped nearly half an hour. He needed to use the bathroom and sure hoped they'd get down soon.

Next to him, Kelly snuggled in close. There were goosebumps on her arms and he rubbed them. Then he realized she'd said something.

"What?" he asked.

"I said, do you believe in second chances?"

"For some things, yeah," he answered, his eyes fixed to the crowd below. "I mean, look at sports teams. How many of those guys have been given a second chance? Maybe it was on that team, maybe it was being drafted to another team. Either way, it was a second chance. As a matter of fact, last season—"

She put her hand over his mouth. "Us, Brett. I'm talking about us," Kelly said, in an exasperated tone as she moved her hand away. "Do you think *we* can have a second chance?"

"Oh. I knew that," Brett said.

"Suuuuure." She smirked at him.

He had. But he didn't want to give in to her so easily. It wasn't payback, exactly, but he couldn't resist teasing her a little.

But when he looked down at her, something in her eyes made him grow serious. Brett reached his free hand to

Kelly's cheek and slid his fingers down her silky skin. She never moved her eyes from his.

"I do," he finally answered.

Kelly didn't say anything, just kept looking at him. He could tell her mind was going a thousand miles an hour. She was thinking about what to say, how to say it, how not to mess anything up. If this wasn't the moment he'd been waiting for almost five years for, he'd have laughed at her expressions.

Instead, he leaned in, closing the distance between them in an instant. His lips found hers at the exact moment the sky lit up with fireworks.

Startled, they pulled apart and looked up.

"Woah. I could not have done that any better if I'd planned it," Brett said.

Kelly laughed. She pulled him close in for another kiss as the Ferris wheel groaned and slowly started to move.

"We're free!" she gasped a moment later as they exited the ride. She squeezed his hand and said, "I've got to pee. Like, so bad."

"Same," Brett said, heading toward the restrooms.

A glance over his shoulder showed the other trapped members of the ride were close behind.

"Hustle, or they'll be a line," he warned.

Her laugher filled his ears as she broke into a jog, Brett right behind her.

A few minutes later, they cheered and applauded with the rest of the crowd as the fireworks show ended.

"Too bad it's over," Brett said, as they walked home, using the flashlight on his cellphone for light. "I love the fair."

Kelly's fingers were laced with his. "Endings aren't always bad," she said. "Sometimes they lead to new, better, beginnings, because you appreciate them more."

"Is that the case with us?" Brett asked, as they turned onto their street.

Kelly didn't answer. When he looked down to see why she hadn't spoken, she reached up on her tiptoes, her free hand tucking behind his neck, and pulled him in close. "I love you," she whispered.

Brett couldn't help but grin. "I love you too," he said.

In the distance, he could see the porch lights were on his house, and his parents and Kelly's were in the section of the yard that connected. "Come on. Let's go share the news," Brett said.

Kelly wrapped his arm around her. "Bet you they already know."

"Bet you a sandwich from Sergio's it's a surprise," he countered.

"You're on," Kelly said.

Brett laughed, and as they drew close, he saw their parents all smiling at them. He gave a groan.

"I'll take mine with a side of fries," Kelly told him. "See you tomorrow for lunch." She kissed him soundly on the lips, waved goodnight, and ran inside.

Brett stood there for a moment, then turned, grinning. This was one second chance he was looking forward to.

Epilogue

Two years later

Kelly stood, peering through the window that overlooked her parents' garden. Her dad's flowers were at their finest, and dozens of chairs were sitting in rows, filled with friends and family, laughing and talking amongst themselves.

It was hard to believe everything that had happened. At times, it felt almost like a dream. She and Brett had tentatively started dating again after the fair. It was as if they'd never been separated. A few months later, he asked her to marry him, and of course, she said yes.

About the same time, a construction company nearby contacted her dad, and asked if he'd be willing to come on as a consultant. He hadn't stopped smiling since the day he'd left the hardware store.

Kelly and Brett had found a cute little house almost halfway between her job, where she was now a full real estate agent, and his, where he was up for promotion in his department. It wasn't too far away from Pumpkin City, either, so they'd be able to visit their parents often as well.

Through the window, she could hear the faint strains of piano music. Mildred down the street was an excellent player, and had offered to play for everyone as well as share some of her prize-winning flowers from that year's fair for Kelly's decorations. With some difficulty, a piano had been brought into the garden, and pots of her bright orange-red prairie lilies dotted the yard, a beautiful compliment to her father's late blooming white peonies.

"Ready, pumpkin?" her dad asked.

Kelly turned around and nodded. "Ready, Dad," she said, and took his arm.

Together they walked down the stairs and out into the yard, where the guests rose as the "Wedding March" began to play. Before she realized it, Kelly was at the front of the crowd, with Megan in her bridesmaid dress next to her beaming.

Everything next felt a blur, until the preacher pronounced her and Brett husband and wife. They walked back down the aisle, and were instantly surrounded by guests. Kelly was pretty sure her heart would burst from the love she felt from friends, family, and from Brett.

As she threw her bouquet, a young woman caught it and squealed, "I get a second chance!"

Kelly laughed. She couldn't help it. Pumpkin City sure was a place with second chances. She was proof of that.

Brett's arm wrapped around her waist and she leaned into him. "Ready to go?" he asked.

She nodded, and they ran to his truck as everyone cheered and waved goodbye.

As they rode down the highway, the radio going in and out with static, Kelly looked over and smiled. "Are you ready to—Look out!"

Brett hit the brakes as a cow wandered into the road. It looked at them, chewed its cud, and slowly walked across to the other side.

Laughing, Kelly said, "Only here."

"One of the many charms about Pumpkin City," Brett grinned as they continued down the road. "Ready for our next adventure?"

Kelly slipped her sunglasses on. "Ready. Whatever it is, I know I'm going to love it."

"You don't even know what I have planned," Brett said, looking over at her.

"I don't have to," she answered. "I'm going to love it, because I'm with you."

Thank you for taking the time to read Second Chance in Pumpkin City!

Could I ask for one small favor? Reviews like yours on Amazon mean so much to me and help others to find my books! Even just a single line means a lot!

Stop by my website to see everything I've written and keep up to date! Join my newsletter for exclusive sneak peeks and surprises.

www.sarahlambbooks.com

About the Author

Sarah Lamb is the mother of two boys and wife to a teacher. She spends her days writing in the beautiful Shenandoah Valley.

She also writes non-fiction books, with an emphasis on self-advocacy and food allergy awareness, as well as books for middle grade and young adult readers.

Want more of Sarah's books? Here are just a few. Find them all on Amazon!

Caroline (Runaway Brides of the West Series)

The Christmas Treasure (Holiday Cottage Series)

Mathilda (Rescue Me: Mail-order Brides Series)

Louise (Rescue Me: Mail-order Brides Series)

Frances (Women of the Blue Ridge Series)

Second Chance in Pumpkin City (Pumpkin City Series)

A Gunslinger for Grace (Mail Order Papa Series)

An Angel for Alice (A Christmas Eve short story)

A Second Chance for Beatrice (A Christmas Eve short story)